PRiNCE NOT-SO CHARMiNG

The Prince Not-So Charming series

Once Upon a Prank

Her Royal Slyness

The Dork Knight

Happily Ever Laughter

Toad You So!

PRINCE NOT-SO CHARMING

Toad You So!

Roy L. Hinuss

Illustrated by Matt Hunt

[Imprint]
MAKE YOUR MARK

New York

[Imprint]
MAKE YOUR MARK

A part of Macmillan Publishing Group, LLC
175 Fifth Avenue, New York, NY 10010

PRINCE NOT-SO CHARMING: TOAD YOU SO!. Copyright © 2019 by
Imprint. All rights reserved. Printed in the United States of America by
LSC Communications, Harrisonburg, Virginia.

Library of Congress Cataloging-in-Publication Data is available.

ISBN 978-1-250-14246-7 (paperback) / ISBN 978-1-250-14245-0 (ebook)

Our books may be purchased in bulk for promotional, educational, or
business use. Please contact your local bookseller or the Macmillan
Corporate and Premium Sales Department at (800) 221-7945 ext. 5442 or
by e-mail at MacmillanSpecialMarkets@macmillan.com.

Book design by Ellen Duda

Illustrations by Matt Hunt

Imprint logo designed by Amanda Spielman

First edition, 2019

1 3 5 7 9 10 8 6 4 2

mackids.com

Don't swipe this book, 'cause here's the deal:
A curse will hit you with great zeal.
You'll grow a zit you can't conceal.
Your scabs will never, ever heal.
You'll ouch and ache from head to heel.
You won't *believe* how bad you'll feel!
So please take heed and hear my spiel.
Please *buy* this book instead of steal.

For Lady Meg and Lady Ellen.

May the evil spell upon you be broken soon.

CHAPTER 1

Prince Carlos Charles Charming was trapped inside a box he couldn't see.

He pressed his palms against one of the box's invisible walls. It was as solid as a rock. The other walls were solid, too. He pounded his fist against the top of the box, then

rammed his shoulder against it. But nothing budged.

Jack the Jester sat crisscross applesauce on the floor a few feet away. He watched Carlos struggle.

"You're stuck now, young'un!" Jack said. A smirk stretched across his brown, wrinkled cheeks. "How does that make you feel?"

Carlos's eyes went wide with panic. He continued to search and struggle against every inch of the invisible box. Maybe he could find a weakness. There *had* to be a weakness.

Jack's smile grew wider. "Let's see how

you handle yourself when those walls start closing in."

As if the box could hear Jack's words, the walls began to push in on all sides. Carlos was forced into a crouch. He shoved and elbowed and punched and kicked, but the walls kept pressing in, closer and closer.

Carlos scrunched his body into a tight, uncomfortable ball. His eyes squinted shut.

He used his last ounce of strength to take a deep breath. He opened his mouth as wide as it could go and let out an anguished scream.

But no sound came out. Not a scream, not a whimper, not a peep. *Nothing!*

Jack leapt to his feet. The old jester clapped wildly.

"Wow! What a performance!" he exclaimed.

Carlos smiled. Then he stood up. He was no longer in the invisible box. Because there *was* no invisible box. It was all just an act.

"I was good?" Carlos asked.

"Good?!" Jack exclaimed. "Are you *kidding* me? I think you were a mime in a past life! You were so good, I was ready to rescue you from a box that wasn't even there!"

"Thanks, Jack." Carlos beamed.

"Don't thank *me*," Jack said. "Thank *you* for making my teaching job so much fun." Jack scratched his gray-whiskered chin. "Dang. I think you mimed just about *everything* today. Let's see. . . . You got crushed inside an imaginary box. . . ."

"I pulled on an imaginary rope . . . ," Carlos said.

"You leaned on an imaginary countertop . . . ," Jack said.

"I juggled imaginary torches . . . ," Carlos said.

"And you burned yourself on those imaginary torches," Jack said. "That was a nice detail."

"*And* I rode an imaginary unicycle *while* ironing an imaginary pair of polyester pants *while* eating an imaginary taco salad," Carlos said.

"I'm still not sure how you pulled that one off," Jack said. "You've got this mime thing down, young'un. You've got this *down*."

"Thanks!" Carlos's happy gaze flickered to the far wall of the Fancy Castle ballroom. The ticking grandfather clock read 4:30 P.M.

"Holy schmoley!" Carlos exclaimed. "My jester lesson went two hours longer than usual!"

"Is that a problem?" Jack asked with a cheery glint in his eye.

7

"Of course not!" Carlos replied. "I'd do jester lessons *forever* if Mom and Dad let me."

Jestering was Carlos's passion, but he also had a day job. Carlos was prince of the happy and peaceful land of Faraway Kingdom. His mom and dad, Queen Cora and King Carmine, were the kingdom's rulers.

Queen Cora and King Carmine were wonderful and fair rulers. They were also wonderful and fair parents—but no parent is perfect. The king and queen often interrupted Carlos's jester lessons to make him do his princely chores.

Oh, how Carlos *hated* princely chores.

But not today! For the first time in

forever, the king and queen had let Carlos jester the entire afternoon away. Because he'd had more time than usual to practice his jestering, Carlos had been able to mime anything and everything.

"Holy schmoley," Carlos said again. "This is turning out to be a really good day."

◆　◆　◆

Carlos practically skipped down the long hallway of Fancy Castle. His jingle-toed jester shoes jingled merrily.

From the opposite direction, Carlos spotted two people walking toward him. One was tall and lanky. The other was short and round. The tall, lanky person was his dad, King Carmine. The short, round person was his mom, Queen Cora.

Oh, well, Carlos thought with a sigh. *All really good days must come to an end. Mom and Dad are going to make me do something princely, like explore the haunted mountains or chase ruthless pirates or cut the ribbon for a new Faraway Kingdom used-horse dealership.*

"Hello, my babycakes!" Queen Cora chirped, wearing a huge smile on her glowing, tan face. (The queen *always* wore a huge smile on her glowing, tan face.) She stretched out her arms and swept Carlos into a big, strong, squeezy hug. "Are you having a good day, sweetie?" she asked.

"Mumphf-humphf," Carlos gasped. (It was the best reply he could come up with. The queen's big, strong, squeezy hugs made it difficult for him to breathe.)

"How was the jester lesson?" asked King Carmine. He wore a smile, too. This was unusual. The king's many responsibilities often twisted his mouth into a frown. The king was always a kind, loving, and patient father, but he was kind, loving, and patient in a frowny way.

"Mumps a humph a wuhmuh," Carlos replied. (He was still being hugged.)

King Carmine turned to the queen. "Sweetie, let the boy breathe."

"Oh, but I love him more than anything!" she sang, making her hug a little tighter than before.

"Gah!" Carlos cried out between gasping gurgles.

"I know how much you love Carlos," the king said, "but he's turning blue."

"Oh! Goodness!" The queen released Carlos from her grasp. "Are you okay, my angel?"

In between wheezes, Carlos nodded.

The king patiently waited for Carlos's blue skin to fade away. Once it did, the king repeated his question.

"So how was the jester lesson, son?"

"It was great," Carlos said. "Do you need me for something, Dad?"

"No," the king replied.

Carlos's eyes went wide. "No? Really? You don't need me to do anything princely?"

"No," the king repeated. "We don't need anything."

"Nothing?" Carlos asked. "You guys need *nothing at all*?"

"Nothing at all!" announced the delighted queen. "You've been doing so *many* excellent princely things lately. Your father and I thought you could use a day off!"

Carlos couldn't believe his ears. "Really?!"

"Yes! Really!" the queen giggled.

The king's smile stretched wider across his lined, tan face. "There's a ribbon cutting for a new Faraway Kingdom used-horse dealership, but your mother and I will take care of that."

"Oh, how I love ribbon cuttings! The ribbon is always so beautiful!" the queen cried. "Can I do the cutting part?"

"Of course you may," the king replied.

"Those giant scissors are just so silly! So

fun!" the queen said. "Aren't they silly and fun, Carmine?"

"Yes, I suppose they are," the king replied. He turned to Carlos. "Enjoy the rest of your day, son."

Carlos watched in wonder as his parents continued their long walk down the hall.

"Holy schmoley," Carlos said. "This is turning out to be a *great* day!"

◆ ◆ ◆

It was almost dinnertime, and Carlos could feel his stomach twitch and grumble. He decided to pay a visit to the Fancy Castle chef.

The aroma coming from the kitchen was not very inviting. It reminded Carlos of the time he left his sneakers out in the rain.

He poked his head through the kitchen doorway. Inside, the air was as hot and humid as a swamp. At once a trickle of sweat dribbled down Carlos's back. He squinted through the steamy fog rising from dozens of bubbling pots.

"Chef Auskotzen?" he called out.

A loud voice with a thick German accent called back, "Yah? Who's zere?"

"It's me, Carlos!"

"Carlos!" Chef Auskotzen leapt out from behind a copper pot large enough to bathe a hippo. He was a tiny man but solidly built, like a steel barrel full of pickles. He wore a grin that stretched all the way across his red, freckled face. "Hallo, young prince!"

"What's for supper?" Carlos asked.

"My specialty!" came the chef's joyous reply. "Toad Surprise!"

"Ew," Carlos muttered under his breath.

But Carlos's "ew" was drowned out by another, more emotional "EW!"

This "EW!" was so close to Carlos's ear—
and so dang *loud*—that it made the young
jester stumble sideways into a wall.

Carlos turned his startled gaze to the source of the "EW!"

Standing a few feet away was Smudge, Fancy Castle's resident dragon.

Dragons do not usually live in castles. But Smudge was not a usual dragon. Most dragons were violent and ferocious. Smudge preferred snuggles and belly rubs. Most dragons used their fiery breath to burn down villages. Smudge used his fiery breath to light chandeliers and toast marshmallows. Most dragons ate villagers. Smudge was on a meatless diet. (Luckily, as Smudge often observed, there's no meat in ice cream.)

In short, Smudge was a *perfect* resident dragon. He was the size of a grizzly bear but as happy as a goat on a trampoline.

"Oh, hai, CC!" Smudge exclaimed. "Did I surprise you?"

Carlos peeled himself off the wall. "Yes," he said. "You really did!"

"YAY!" Smudge flapped his rubbery bat-like wings with glee. "My sneaking booties work!"

Carlos peered down at Smudge's feet. The dragon was wearing a pair of thick, pink wool slippers.

Smudge giggled. "I knitted these booties to keep my toenails from going

clickita-clickita on the floor! So I can be sneaky. I knitted the booties extra, extra thick because my toenails are superduper long."

That was another thing that made Smudge different from other dragons: He was an accomplished knitter.

Carlos gave Smudge a scratch under his chin. "Those booties sure worked on me."

"YAY!" Smudge said again.

Then the dragon's voice suddenly became grumpy. "Today would be the *perfect* day if we weren't getting toads for supper."

"I don't want to eat toads, either," Carlos said.

"Toads *scare* me," Smudge added.

"They *scare* you?" Carlos asked.

Smudge nodded, his eyes wide with fright. "Yes! They're tiny and slimy, and their bref is so cold and damp!"

Carlos thought for a moment. He leaned

close to Smudge's ear. "I know a way to make this day perfect," he whispered.

"You do?" Smudge whispered back.

"I've been hiding desserts in my room for just such an emergency," Carlos whispered.

"You have?" Smudge whispered back— a little louder this time.

"We can have a supper of cupcakes," Carlos whispered.

"WE CAN?!" Smudge no longer felt like whispering.

"Yes, we can!" Carlos didn't feel like whispering, either.

"Ooh, CC! I'm so excited! I gotta go do

dragon tinkles!" Smudge hopped up and down—partly because he was excited and partly because he really did have to tinkle. "I'll go to the potty and then meet you in your room!"

Carlos watched his dragon friend skitter off down the hall.

"Holy schmoley," Carlos sighed. "This is turning out to be a *perfect* day."

◆ ◆ ◆

Carlos trotted to his room. He'd been smiling for so long that his face was starting to ache.

It was a happy-face ache that Carlos never wanted to end.

But it did.

Quickly.

The happiness ended the moment Carlos pushed open the door to his room.

Standing along the far wall, near an open window, was a skeleton of a man. His gray hair was long and straight, his skin as pale as paper. He was wrapped from shoulder to shinbones in wrinkled black robes.

"Who are you?" Carlos asked sternly. "What are you doing in my room?"

"I am the great and powerful Weatherwax," the man replied in a high-pitched,

raspy voice. "I am a sorcerer for hire. And I am here on a job."

"A job?" Carlos asked. "What job?"

"My job is to put a curse on you," Weather-wax replied.

"A curse?" Carlos asked. "On ME?!"

Before Carlos could say another word, he was overwhelmed by a cloud of thick, stinging smoke.

CHAPTER 2

When Carlos finally blinked the smoke from his eyes, he found Weatherwax still standing by the open window. The sorcerer's arms were crossed. His face wore a smug smile of triumph.

Carlos coughed. "What did you just do?"

"I turned you into a toad," Weatherwax replied with a sharp laugh.

Carlos looked himself over. Nothing had changed. He was still a prince in a jester suit. "I'm not a toad."

"Yes, you are," Weatherwax insisted. "Just not *yet*. I brew my spells with a delayed reaction. You will turn into a toad in exactly"—he glanced at his wristwatch—"ninety seconds. I make my spells that way so my victims can ask me a few questions before they get all ribbit-y."

Carlos's eyes grew wide. "I'm feeling a tingling in my feet."

Weatherwax nodded. "That's the spell working its magic."

A jolt of fear shot up Carlos's spine. "Someone hired you to do this to me?" he squeaked out.

"Yup," Weatherwax replied.

"Who?!" Carlos could feel the tingling sensation begin to creep up his legs.

"Your worst enemy!" Weatherwax boomed.

Carlos searched his memory for worst enemies.

"Queen Cayenne?" Carlos asked.

"No."

"Sir Lance A. Lott?" Carlos asked.

"No!"

"Cornelius the horse?" Carlos asked.

"NO!" Weatherwax was getting impatient. "Come on! Everybody should know the name of their worst enemy!"

"Well, I don't!" Carlos cried. The tingling had trickled up to his belly. His nerves were frazzled. "Tell me!"

"Your worst enemy is . . ." Weatherwax paused dramatically. "Sherrie Madrid!"

"Who?" Carlos asked.

"Sherrie Madrid," Weatherwax said again. "You know."

"No, I *don't* know," Carlos replied through

gritted teeth. "Who the heck is Sherrie Madrid?"

"She's your ex-wife," Weatherwax said.

Carlos needed a moment to let the stupidity of that statement sink in.

"MY EX-WIFE?!" Carlos yelled. "I'VE NEVER BEEN MARRIED! LOOK AT ME! I'M A KID!"

Weatherwax's eyebrows crinkled in confusion. "Oh," he said. The sorcerer pulled a dog-eared appointment book from one of the folds in his robe and fumbled through the pages. "Hold on. Hold on a minute."

"A minute?" Carlos roared. "I don't *have* a minute!" The weird tingling had traveled

down both of his arms. Carlos could feel his fingertips tremble.

"Don't . . . don't d-distract me," Weatherwax stammered. "I-I'll get to the bottom of this in just a second. One second."

At last, Weatherwax's finger reached the correct passage in his appointment book. "Ah! Here it is. I was right: Your name is Carlos Charlesbridge."

"No, it's not!" Carlos paced around the room like a starving tiger. "I'm Carlos Charles Charming!"

"Are you a plumber?" Weatherwax asked.

"I'm a *prince*!"

"Uh-oh," Weatherwax said.

Carlos took a deep breath to calm himself, but the tingles had now settled heavily into his lungs. "Okay. You made a mistake. You can see that now. So just reverse the spell and get out of here."

"Um . . . ," Weatherwax began.

Carlos knew that good news *never* begins with "um."

"'Um'? Did you say 'um'?" Carlos, now tingling from head to toe, stormed up to Weatherwax. "Why did you say 'um'?"

Weatherwax grew even paler than he already was. "Because I . . . um . . . um . . . um."

"No more um-ing!" Carlos grabbed Weatherwax's robes and yanked the tall sorcerer down toward the ground. They were now nose-to-nose. "What's wrong?"

Weatherwax began to babble. "I don't know how to reverse the spell!" he blubbered. "I'm hired to turn people *into* things! No one ever hires me to turn them *back*! I never learned to do the turning-back part! I missed that day in sorcery school! I had a bellyache! The instructor told me to copy someone's notes, but the lesson wasn't going to be on the midterm, so I never did! I know that's no excuse! I know I should've shown more appreciation for the learning process! But I was young and foolish! And I'm sorry! I'm really, really sorry!"

The tingling overwhelmed Carlos now.

Oh, no, Carlos thought.

Carlos felt his muscles constrict. He felt his mouth stretch and his eyes bulge.

Oh, no! Carlos thought.

And Carlos saw himself shrink . . .

. . . and shrink . . .

. . . and shrink . . .

. . . until he barely came up to Weatherwax's ankles.

OH, NO! Carlos thought.

And then the toad warts popped up.

Ew, Carlos thought.

Weatherwax looked down at Carlos the toad. "I'm sorry," Weatherwax said. "I'd help you if I could, but, um, I gotta find this plumber guy. So . . . take it easy."

Carlos watched helplessly as Weatherwax disappeared through the bedroom window.

Carlos stared at his webbed toes. He sighed. The sigh made the skin under his chin swell up like an icky, warty, brownish-green balloon.

Ew, Carlos thought.

He didn't know what to do next, so he did nothing.

Until he heard a happy song echo outside of his bedroom door.

"It's a great, great day to eat cup-cupcaaaakes with my bestest, bestest friend!"

Smudge! Carlos thought. *Smudge will help me!*

The door to the room burst open.

"Hey, CC! I'm ready for my cupcakes!" Smudge declared.

"Smudge!" Carlos shouted. "It's me! Carlos! I need your help! A sorcerer turned me into a toad, and I need to figure out a way to break the spell!"

Actually, Carlos *didn't* shout that.

Carlos *wanted* to shout that. He *tried* to

shout that. But when the words reached his mouth, they came out as:

"Ribbit!"

A fireball of terror exploded from Smudge's mouth. "Gah!" he screamed. "An icky toad! With cold, damp bref!"

Smudge, his wool booties slipping and sliding on the stone floor, scrambled back through the bedroom door and down the hall as fast as his feet would carry him.

"WAIT! SMUDGE, WAIT!" Carlos cried.

But the words came out as "RIBBIT!"

Carlos rubbed his toad eyes. *Why on earth is a huge, fire-breathing dragon afraid of a tiny little toad?* he grumped.

But Carlos knew the answer didn't matter. Smudge was afraid, and there was nothing Carlos could do about it.

"This day is actually turning out to be surprisingly awful," Carlos muttered.

But the words came out as "Ribbit."

CHAPTER 3

Leaping like a toad wasn't nearly as fun as Carlos might have imagined.

Sproing. Carlos leapt.

Bump. Carlos landed on the stone floor.

"Ow, my butt," Carlos whined.

But the words came out as "Ribbit."

And so it went, one leap after the other

down the long, butt-achy stone hallway. Carlos always thought Fancy Castle was too big. But now, with every butt bump, he found Fancy Castle to be *waaaaay* too big.

Sproing. Bump. "Ribbit."

Sproing. Bump. "Ribbit."

Carlos had come up with a plan. Sort of. Carlos's plan was to find his father.

Dad will know what to do, Carlos told himself.

But there was a problem. A big problem. Carlos no longer looked like Carlos. And Carlos could no longer talk. What would Carlos do once he found his dad? How could he explain what happened? Would his dad recognize him? Or would the king think Carlos was just a toad?

Dad will know who I am, Carlos thought. *At least, I hope so.*

There was another problem with Carlos's plan: Carlos had to hurry. The king and queen would be leaving the castle any minute for the ribbon-cutting ceremony.

So Carlos leapt toward the throne room a bit faster than before.

Sproing! Bump! "Ribbit!"

Sproing! Bump! "Ribbit!"

Sproing! Bump! "Ri—"

Carlos froze. A few yards down the hall, a tired maid was leaning heavily on the handle of her mop.

What will she do if she sees me? Carlos wondered.

I'd better not move, he thought. *Because if I* do *move and she* does *see me, she might freak out.*

So Carlos didn't move.

But the maid saw him anyway.

And she freaked out.

"EEEK!"

She grabbed her mop handle like it was a giant mallet and started to swing.

With lightning reflexes, Carlos sprang sideways just as the mop crashed down on the spot where he had been squatting.

Carlos sproinged past the charging maid and hopped down the hallway as fast as he could.

*SPROINGBUMP*RIBBIT!

*SPROINGBUMP*RIBBIT!

*SPROINGBUMP*RIBBIT!

But the maid was hot on his heels. Her mop hammered the ground.

It was quite a ruckus. Doors swung open. Servants poked their heads into the hall.

"Toad loose in the castle! Toad loose in the castle!" the maid screeched. "And it's a fast one!"

A few servants screamed in terror. Others screamed with laughter. But every single one of them joined the chase.

Why does everyone in this castle hate toads so much? Carlos wondered.

The mob of running footsteps rumbled like thunder. Carlos didn't look over his shoulder to see how close they were getting,

but it sounded like they were getting *very* close.

Very, *very* close.

What am I going to do? Carlos thought. His cold, damp breath caught in his throat. *I need a place to hide!*

Carlos skidded around a sharp corner

and spotted a plain wooden door with rusty hinges. He squished himself under the door.

Moments later, the mob raced around the bend, past the door, and down the long hallway.

Carlos waited until the sounds of the tromping footsteps had faded away.

Once the hall fell silent, Carlos flopped onto his toad belly. He panted and wheezed. Through tired, blurred eyes, Carlos took in his surroundings. The room was small and messy. The place felt familiar, but Carlos was too exhausted to give it much thought.

Carlos was hungry, too. He hadn't gotten the chance to eat his cupcakes.

But as hungry as Carlos was, he wasn't in the mood for cupcakes.

For the first time in his life, Carlos wondered what a cockroach might taste like.

Ew. A coackroach, Carlos thought. But the "ew" was insincere. Carlos really *did* want a cockroach.

He wanted a cockroach more than anything else in the world.

He scanned the floor, but it was bug-free.

"Dang it!" Carlos said.

But the words came out as "Ribbit!"

The "ribbit" was a little louder than Carlos had expected.

And Carlos was not alone in this tiny, messy room.

"Well, what do we have here?" an amused voice said. A bony fist snapped Carlos up. "It looks like Chef Auskotzen has misplaced his Toad Surprise."

CHAPTER 4

Carlos's large eyes grew a little bit larger.

The man who held Carlos firmly in his strong, bony fist was none other than Jack the Jester.

"Jack!" Carlos shouted. "Boy, am I glad to see you!"

But the words came out as "Ribbit!"

Jack smiled. "You're a cute little fella," he said. "But you're freaking out all the servants. So I'd better get you back to the kitchen."

Carlos's toad neck puffed up in alarm. "Wait! Don't do that!" he shouted. Carlos yanked his tiny toad arms out from under Jack's index finger and flailed them wildly. "It's me! It's Carlos!"

But the words came out as "Ribbit!"

Jack walked to the door and opened it. He strode down the long stone hallway. His jester shoes jingle-jangled with every step.

"I'm not dinner! I'm a jester!" Carlos cried. "I'll prove it! Gimme something to juggle! Gimme a lute to play! Gimme a pencil, and I'll write you a killer poop joke! Gimme some stilts! Wait, no, don't give me stilts. I still haven't nailed the stilts. But gimme anything else that's jestery, and I'll jester the heck out of it!"

But the words came out as "Ribbit!"

Jack kept jingle-jangling to the kitchen. Carlos's nose picked up the faint aroma of rained-on sneakers.

"Come on, Jack!" Carlos cried. "Look at me! You *have* to know who I am! We've been together all ding-dang day! All day long you've been teaching me to . . ."

Carlos gasped. Suddenly an idea popped into his toady brain.

Jack reached the kitchen door. He was about to push it open.

"YOU'VE BEEN TEACHING ME TO MIME!" Carlos shouted.

But the words came out as "RIBBIT!"

The loudness of Carlos's "RIBBIT!" stopped the old jester in his tracks.

Jack regarded the toad he held. The toad was no longer struggling. It was no longer ribbit-ing.

The toad was pressing its warty palms against an invisible wall.

The wall was as solid as a rock. The other walls were solid, too. The toad pounded its fist against the top of the invisible box. The toad rammed its shoulder against it, but nothing budged.

Jack's eyes grew as wide as dinner plates. His mouth dropped open.

"Carlos?" he whispered. "Is that you?"

Carlos nodded.

"Oh, my," he said. "Oh, my!"

Cradling the toad gently in both hands, Jack raced back to his small, messy room. Once they were inside, he bolted the door.

"Carlos!" Jack said. "I'm so sorry, kiddo!"

Jack didn't usually hug much, but he

couldn't help himself this time. Jack hugged Carlos so hard that Carlos's long, sticky tongue flopped out of his mouth.

"RIBBIT!" he protested angrily. Carlos wriggled loose and leapt onto the straw mattress Jack used for a bed.

"Oh! Sorry, young'un. Didn't mean to hug you so hard." Jack looked at his feet in embarrassment. "I'm just really glad you're okay." Jack sat crisscross applesauce on the floor beside the bed. "How did this all happen?" he asked.

Carlos balanced upon his spindly toad legs and told the story in the only way he knew how: by miming.

Ten minutes later, Jack finally spoke. "So let me get this straight. You were going to have cupcakes in your room, but a sorcerer was there, and he turned you into a toad because he thought you were a plumber with an angry ex-wife named Sherrie Madrid. Smudge finds you, but he runs away because he is frightened by toad 'bref.' So you decide to search out the king, but on your way to the throne room, a maid sees you and tries to whack you with a mop. And before you know it, other servants are coming from everywhere to chase you. And that's when you squeezed under my door. Did I get all that right?"

Carlos nodded.

"Dang, you're a good mime," Jack said.

Carlos couldn't help but smile.

Jack sprang to his feet. "Okay, then. Your mom and dad won't be back for a while, so it's up to us to figure out how to break this spell." Jack strode to his cluttered shelves and scanned their dusty contents. "Fortunately, I have a book that will help. I've done some sorcery studies in my day. A good jester must know a little bit about everything."

Jack plucked an especially fat, tattered volume from the shelf and laid it upon the straw mattress so Carlos could read along. When Jack opened the cover, the book's spine cracked and crunched in protest.

"If the answer is anywhere, it's in here," Jack said with a confident nod. "And if the answer *isn't* here . . . then there *is* no answer."

CHAPTER 5

Carlos and Jack had been skimming the book for nearly twenty minutes when Jack stabbed a paragraph with his index finger. The finger stab stirred up a cloud of moldy dust that made them both sneeze.

Jack read from the yellowed page: "'To break the frog spell, the cursed prince must find a princess who he loves with the warmth of one thousand suns.'"

Oh, no, Carlos thought.

Jack continued reading. "'And this prin-

cess must, in turn, love the be-frogged prince even more—with the warmth of two thousand suns.'"

Oh, no! Carlos thought.

Unfortunately, Jack had more to read. "'And the prince and the princess must kiss on the lips.'"

Oh, NO! Carlos thought.

"'And this lip kiss must burn with the passion of four thousand suns.'"

"Oh, come ON!" Carlos sputtered, flailing his arms. "I don't love a princess with the warmth of one thousand suns! And I don't know a princess who loves *me* with the warmth of *two* thousand suns! And how the heck does *one* thousand suns plus *two* thousand suns equal *four* thousand suns? The math is all screwed up!" Carlos covered his mouth in horror. "And kissing?! On the *lips*?! EW! I don't want to kiss anybody! Kissing is gross! It's the grossest thing in the history of grossness!"

But the words came out as "Ribbit!"

Carlos could've gone on and on and on about how gross kisses were, but he was too distracted by a nearby cockroach. Before Carlos could give it a second thought, he shot out his sticky tongue and slurped the twitching insect into his mouth.

Mm! Tasty! Carlos thought.

"Look, kiddo, I get it," Jack said. "You're not into the kissing thing yet. But this is the only way." Jack paused a moment to let the reality of the situation sink in. "So . . . ," he continued, "how do you feel about kissing Princess Pinky?"

Princess Pinky lived in the neighboring kingdom of Ever-After Land. She hated princess training almost as much as Carlos hated prince training. She was one of Carlos's best friends. But Carlos did *not* love her with the warmth of one thousand suns. And he was certain Pinky didn't love him with the warmth of two thousand suns. At least, he *hoped* she didn't. And the idea of

kissing Pinky—*on the lips!*—with the passion of four thousand suns made Carlos a little queasy.

"So what do you say, kiddo?" Jack asked. "It might work."

Carlos sighed. His warty neck puffed up.

Carlos didn't want to be a toad. And if he had to kiss someone, it might as well be Pinky.

Carlos nodded unhappily. The kiss had to happen.

Jack nodded back. He jingle-jangled to his wardrobe, reached for a patchwork cloak, and threw it around his shoulders. "Okay, young'un. I'll go get Pinky. You sit tight here

until I get back. I'll lock the door behind me.
Don't move. Don't make a sound. Got it?"

Carlos got it.

Jack dashed from the room and locked
Carlos inside.

"Please hurry," Carlos whispered.

But the words came out as "Ribbit."

CHAPTER 6

Why didn't Jack take me with him? Carlos thought.

It was the kind of thought a person thinks after it's too late to do anything.

But if there was one place Carlos would *choose* to hide, it would be in Jack's room. It was a dusty, messy place, but it was also a jester's paradise. To pass the time, Carlos decided to explore. He sprang from the bed and landed on the hard stone floor.

"Ow, my butt!" Carlos said.

But the words came out as "Ribbit!"

Shush! Carlos thought. *I can't make noise! If anyone knows I'm here, I'll end up as Toad Surprise!*

Carlos leapt again, this time keeping the "Ow, my butt!" to himself. He moved across the room—sidestepping the fake dog poop, playing cards, and juggling pins—until he reached Jack's huge wooden trunk. Carlos had never explored the trunk before, but he had often seen Jack dig into it. Every time

Jack unlatched the lid, Carlos would do his best to peek inside. He never saw much, but what little he did see looked *awesome*.

Colorful stuff.

Springy stuff.

Clacky, clattery, cling-clangy stuff.

"No peeking, kiddo," Jack would scold in his gentle, good-humored way. "Every jester needs a few secrets!"

Carlos agreed with this. Every jester *should* have a few secrets.

Carlos thought for a moment. *But wait. What's my jester secret?*

As far as Carlos knew, he didn't have any.

Carlos's only secret was that some dumb sorcerer had turned him into a toad.

And Jack knew that secret.

Since Jack knows my *secret,* Carlos's toad logic continued, *I should learn a couple of Jack's secrets! It's only fair.*

(It should be noted that toad logic isn't always logical.)

Carlos began to fumble with the trunk's metal latch, but Carlos's fingers were too floppy and flippery to undo it.

"Dang it," Carlos muttered.

But the words came out as "Ribbit."

Shush! Carlos thought.

From out in the hall, he heard clicking footsteps. And voices.

Carlos froze. He held his breath. He tried to listen over the terrified thumping of his heart.

"I can't believe that toad got away from us," said the first voice.

"Yeah," said the second voice.

"But we'll catch it," said the first voice.

"Yeah," said the second voice.

"We can't have toads running around the castle," said the first voice.

"Yeah," said the second voice.

"I think you meant to say no," said the first voice. "As in, 'No, we *can't* have toads running around the castle.' Did you mean to say no?"

"Yeah," said the second voice.

"Chef Auskotzen knows that one of his toads got away," said the first voice.

"Yeah," said the second voice.

"And Chef Auskotzen told me that he would get the best nose in the castle to sniff out where that toad is hiding," said the first voice.

"Yeah?" asked the second voice.

"Yeah," said the first voice.

Carlos remained completely still until the voices and footsteps disappeared down the hall.

Carlos's brain began to panic. *I have to hide!*

Carlos attacked the latch with new energy. He no longer cared about the mysteries that were hidden inside Jack's trunk. He now only saw the trunk as a pretty good place to hide *himself*.

He pulled the latch. He yanked it. Pushed it. Jiggled it. Slapped it. Swatted it.

And then he stared at it angrily.

"I hate these toad fingers!" Carlos shouted.

But the words came out as "Ribbit!"

"And I hate everything!" Carlos shouted.

But the words came out as "Ribbit!"

"Stop talking!" Carlos scolded himself.

But the words came out as "Ribbit!"

With a roar of frustration, Carlos grabbed a juggling pin off of the floor and used it to bang the latch with all of his might.

Over and over and over again.

And with each *BANG*, he ribbited at the top of his lungs.

"This is turning out . . ." ("Ribbit . . .")

BANG!

". . . to be . . ." (". . . ribbit . . .")

BANG!

". . . the WORST . . ." (". . . RIBBIT . . .")

BANG!

"... DAY ..." ("... RIBBIT ...")

BANG!

"... EVER!" ("... RIBBIT!")

BANG!

Click!

Carlos gasped. He did it! He opened the trunk!

And in that tiny moment of good fortune, Carlos realized that he had been really, *really* loud.

Oh, fart, he thought.

Carlos didn't move a muscle. He listened very carefully.

All was quiet.

Is it possible that no one heard all the noise I made? he wondered.

Carlos listened some more. All was still quiet.

It is possible! Carlos thought. *I can't believe it! No one heard all the noise I made!*

"Did you hear all ze noise zat toad made?" came a distant voice.

Oh, fart, Carlos thought.

He recognized the voice immediately. It belonged to Chef Auskotzen.

The chef's remark was followed by another voice. "I did! I did hear the toad noise, Chef Kittenz!"

That voice belonged to Smudge.

Oh, no! Carlos gulped. *Smudge has the best nose in the castle! Smudge is helping the chef find me!*

"Ze noises came from zat hall," the chef continued. "So sniff under doors for toad smells!"

"But toads frighten me!" Smudge said.

"Vould you rather have a toad running loose in ze castle?"

"No," Smudge admitted.

"Zen ve must catch it!" Chef Auskotzen said. "Don't vorry; I von't let it come near you."

"Okay, Chef Kittenz," Smudge said.

"And stop calling me Kittenz!" Chef Auskotzen grouched.

"But Kittenz is so much better than . . . um . . . whatever your name is," Smudge explained. "Because kittens are lovely and cuddly!"

"Just get sniffin'!" the chef commanded.

"I'll be sniffin', Kittenz," said Smudge.

Carlos heard Smudge sniff and snuffle down the hall.

With every step, Smudge and Chef Auskotzen drew closer and closer to Jack's room.

CHAPTER 7

Hide! I've got to hide! Carlos thought. He sprang into the trunk.

He landed on some chattering teeth.

The teeth bit his butt.

"Ow, my b—"

Carlos slapped his hands over his mouth before the "ribbit" could escape.

Carlos shut the trunk lid just as Smudge's nose appeared under Jack's door.

Carlos peeked through the trunk's key-hole. He saw Smudge's breath blow dust bunnies this way and that. Then he heard Smudge's voice:

"I found it, Chef Kittenz! The toad with the cold, damp bref is in here! But I'm scared! Hold me!"

Carlos heard Chef Auskotzen say "OOF!"

Carlos knew the reason why Chef Auskotzen said "OOF!" It was the same reason most everyone said "OOF" when Smudge was around.

Smudge had a habit of jumping on people when he was frightened.

Smudge also had a habit of jumping on people when he was happy.

Smudge pretty much jumped on people all the time. It was a problem.

"Get off of me!" Chef Auskotzen grunted. "And stop calling me Kittenz!"

With a thunderous crash, Chef Auskotzen kicked in the door to Jack's room. The man's beefy hands held the handle of a butterfly net.

"Here, toady, toady, toady!" the chef said as he shuffled into the room. He pivoted slowly, searching for any signs of movement. "Don't be frightened, little toad!"

"But shouldn't the toad be frightened?" Smudge asked from the hallway. "I mean, you're gonna cook it, right?"

Chef Auskotzen sighed a little. "Yah, Smudge, I am going to cook it."

"Well, if someone was trying to cook *me*, I would be very frightened," Smudge said. "So you shouldn't tell the toad to *not* be frightened, because that would be a fib. And fibbing is wrong."

"Smudge?" Chef Auskotzen said.

"Yes, Chef Kittenz?" Smudge replied.

"Shush."

The chef took another step into the room. And another step. And another. With each step, he moved closer and closer to Jack's trunk. On instinct, Carlos took a small step away from the keyhole.

BRAAAAAAAAP!

Carlos had stepped backward onto a

jewel-encrusted whoopee cushion (a top-of-the-line product from the Hammacher Jester catalog). "Oh, fart," Carlos said.

But the words came out as "Ribbit."

The trunk lid flew open. Before Carlos could react, he was tangled inside the chef's butterfly net.

CHAPTER 8

The toad cage was small. And very, very crowded.

Carlos stared at his five cagemates. And they, with their bulging, blank toad eyes, stared back.

The toad stares began to weird Carlos

out, so he turned his attention to what was going on outside the cage.

Carlos's cage rested on a counter in the castle's kitchen. Chef Auskotzen, nearly hidden behind a fog of steam, happily dumped vegetables into a big, burbling pot.

"Well, this stinks," Carlos sighed.

But the words came out as "Ribbit."

One of the other toads let out a "ribbit," too.

And, much to Carlos's shock, he understood *exactly* what the "ribbit" meant.

"Sorry," the ribbiter had said. "I didn't get a chance to shower today."

Carlos turned toward the direction of the voice. He was, again, face-to-face with the toads.

"Uh," Carlos began, "did you say something?"

"Yeah. You said that something stinks,"

said the first toad. "That would be me. I'm a little pond-scummy today."

"I've got cricket breath," said the second toad.

"And I have punky pits," said the third toad.

"I've got some toad toe jam," said the fourth toad.

"And I farted!" said the fifth toad.

"I can't believe it!" Carlos said in amazement. "I can understand you!"

"Of *course* you can understand us," said the first toad.

"You're a *toad*," said the second toad.

"And you speak fluent Toadese," said the third toad.

"With a slight northern salamander accent," said the fourth toad.

"And I farted!" said the fifth toad.

"Well, I have to get out of this cage," Carlos said. "I'm *not* a toad; I'm a prince!"

If toads had eyebrows, all of the toads would have raised them in disbelief. "A prince? *Suuure* you are," said the first toad.

"I am!" Carlos said. "I'm Prince Carlos Charles Charming. And I'm a jester, too."

"Ooh! A jester prince!" said the second toad.

"La-di-da!" said the third toad.

"Look at the big-time celebrity!" said the fourth toad.

"And I farted!" said the fifth toad.

"We *know* you farted, Gerald. We know!" the first toad groaned. "You've been farting all afternoon! So knock it off!"

The first toad turned back to Carlos. "If you're such a big-deal jester prince, how come I've never heard of you?"

Carlos shrugged, a little embarrassed. "I've never jestered for toads before."

"And you never will," the first toad said. His lower lip began to quiver in fear. "In a couple of minutes, we'll be inside that pot."

The toad was right. Chef Auskotzen was just about ready to start cooking the main course.

Carlos looked upon the five miserable toad faces before him. Never in his life had Carlos seen a group more in need of cheering up.

"Do you guys want to see a little miming?" Carlos asked.

The second toad blinked tears from his bulging eyes. "What's *miming*?" he asked.

"I'll show you," Carlos said.

Carlos trapped himself inside an invisible box.

He pulled on an imaginary rope.

He leaned on an imaginary countertop.

He juggled imaginary torches.

And he rode an imaginary unicycle *while* ironing an imaginary pair of polyester pants *while* eating an imaginary cockroach.

At first, the toads were confused by

Carlos's antics. But that confusion was soon replaced by wide smiles.

"Awesome!" said the first toad.

"Whoa, that's cool!" said the second toad.

"How do you do that?" said the third toad.

"That imaginary cockroach is so convincing!" said the fourth toad.

"I'm still farting," said Gerald, the fifth toad.

The toads began to laugh.

To Carlos, toad laughter was the most beautiful sound he had ever heard. It was bold and melodic, bursting with carefree, innocent joy.

This must be what laughter sounds like in heaven, Carlos thought. *This is amazing!*

And then, in an instant, things *stopped* being amazing.

"Okay, toads! Time for dinner!" Chef Auskotzen lifted the cage off of the counter, swinging and bumping it on his journey to the stewpot.

Carlos and the toads screamed, yelled, and pleaded, but Chef Auskotzen didn't pay any attention. He had a job to do. And that job was to make Toad Surprise.

Chef Auskotzen pried the cage door open.

Toad You So!

Carlos and the toads gripped the wire bars for dear life as the chef shook the cage over the boiling pot.

CHAPTER 9

"Come on, toadies!" Chef Auskotzen said as he shook the cage harder. "Don't be stubborn! Don't be—"

But the chef was interrupted by a strong, bold, booming "STOP!"

It was Jack! The old jester shouted with such kingly authority that Chef Auskotzen froze like a marble statue. In that moment of stillness, Princess Pinky (looking very unlike a princess in her paint-spattered overalls) swooped into the room. She raced to the cage and yanked it from the chef's hands.

"Vait!" Chef Auskotzen protested. "Give me zat! I need to finish dinner!"

"You can finish dinner in a few minutes," Pinky said. "I have a friend in here." She eyed the warty residents of the cage. Pinky's face twisted into a grimace. She turned to Jack. "Are you *sure* I have a friend in here?"

"I'm sure," Jack said.

"Are you *really* sure I have to kiss...," Pinky went on.

"Yes," Jack said.

"On the lips?!" Pinky asked.

"Yes," Jack said again.

"Ew," Pinky said.

Chef Auskotzen scratched his head. "Vy is she kissing ze toads?"

"One of them is Carlos," Jack said. "He's under a sorcerer's spell."

"Carlos?!" The chef covered his mouth in alarm. "Prince Carlos is *a toad*? Oh, no!" Chef Auskotzen looked between the bars of the cage. "Sorry, Carlos, vichever toad you are!"

"Yeah, which one *is* he?" Pinky was still grimacing. "Because I'm not gonna kiss six of these nasty things."

"It's the toad that can mime," Jack said.

Whew! Carlos thought. *This nightmare will soon be over. I just need to mime something.*

Carlos decided to perform the invisible box routine.

But before he could begin, another toad began to mime it.

"Hey, what are you doing?" Carlos exclaimed.

"I'm pretending to be you!" replied the toad. "I don't want to be Toad Surprise!"

"Me, neither!" said the second toad. He pulled an imaginary rope.

"Hey!" Carlos shouted. "You guys are stealing my routine!"

But the toads didn't listen. The third toad leaned on an imaginary counter.

The fourth toad juggled imaginary torches.

And Gerald, the fifth toad, rode an imaginary unicycle *while* ironing a pair of polyester pants *while* eating an imaginary cockroach. While farting.

"Wow!" Jack marveled. "Toads have talent!"

"All except that one," Pinky pointed to Carlos. Carlos wasn't miming at all; he was just standing there in frustration.

Carlos noticed Pinky's gaze. And in that moment, he decided to mime something new.

Carlos mimed climbing the side of an imaginary tower. It was the Tallest Tower, the place where Carlos and Pinky first met.

Next Carlos mimed an artist dabbing imaginary paint onto an imaginary canvas. Pinky was the best artist Carlos had ever seen.

Then Carlos mimed the box step. It was a boring dance, but it was a dance Pinky had taught him, so it wasn't nearly as boring as it *could've* been.

And Carlos kept going. He mimed the games he and Pinky had played together, the pranks they had pulled together, and the many, many adventures they'd shared.

Pinky's eyes went wide with recognition.

As Carlos mimed, he began to feel some-

thing deep inside him that he couldn't quite describe. It wasn't the warmth of one thousand suns. It wasn't *anything* like that. But he could tell the feeling was important.

Very important.

It was, Carlos guessed, the special feeling a person has for a best friend.

Was that love? If so, it was definitely a *nonkissy* love.

But Carlos didn't struggle when Pinky reached into the cage, picked him up, and planted a wet one on his warty lips.

"Ew," Pinky said.

"Ew," Carlos said.

But the word came out as "Ribbit."

CHAPTER 10

Nobody moved. Nobody breathed. The only sound in the kitchen was the murmur of burbling pots.

Carlos waited for the spell to wear off.

Everybody else waited—Pinky, Jack, Chef Auskotzen, and the five toads.

They waited.

And waited.

And waited some more.

They waited for a very long time.

Chef Auskotzen spoke first. "You sure you kissed ze right toad?"

"Yes, I'm sure!" Pinky shot back. "Jack, what's going on here?"

"Looks like nothing is going on," Jack replied.

"I can *see* that!" Pinky used the back of her hand to wipe the toad spit from her lips. "Why isn't Carlos turning into a person?"

"I guess you don't love Carlos with the warmth of two thousand suns," Jack said.

"Wait. *What?*" Pinky cried. "I have to love Carlos with the warmth of *two thousand suns? That's* what we needed to turn him back?"

"That's what the book told me," Jack said.

"Geez, Jack!" she exclaimed. "Kids don't love each other with the warmth of two thousand suns! That would be creepy!"

Chef Auskotzen nodded. "Dat vould be a little creepy," he said.

"Why didn't you *tell* me that I had to love Carlos with the warmth of two thousand suns?" Pinky asked. "Because if you'd *told* me that I needed to love Carlos with the warmth of two thousand suns, I could've told you that I *don't* love Carlos with the warmth of two thousand suns! *And then I wouldn't have had to kiss a toad!*"

Pinky was so annoyed that she sort of forgot she was still holding Carlos. She threw up her hands in irritation, making the toad prince flop and flail around.

"Gah!" Carlos shouted.

But the word came out as "Ribbit!"

"Oh, sorry, Carlos," Pinky said, petting his warty head.

"I thought it was worth a shot." Jack shrugged. "I thought you *might* love him."

Pinky sighed. "I *do* love him—as a best friend. But *that* kind of love is different!"

The news made Carlos's heart happy. *We share a nonkissy love!* he thought.

"I'LL KISS HIM!" someone shouted.

Pinky, Carlos, Jack, Chef Auskotzen, and the toads turned toward the source of the new voice. Standing in the kitchen doorway was Smudge. (Those new sneaking booties worked *really* well.)

"You wanna kiss him?" Jack asked. "I thought you hated toads!"

"I do! But I love CC!" The dragon scampered into the room and used his long, forked tongue to give Carlos a way-too-drippy lick.

"Ew," Carlos said.

But the word came out as "Ribbit."

Smudge pondered the kiss for a long, thoughtful moment.

"Oh! That was nice!" Smudge decided. "You know what? I think I like toads now! I'm gonna kiss CC again!"

Carlos let out a sharp ribbit of protest. Getting the message, Pinky held Carlos a little closer. "Maybe later, Smudge," she said.

Chef Auskotzen glanced at the clock on the kitchen wall. "Ach! It's getting late! Can I cook ze other toads now?"

"No!" Jack exclaimed. "Didn't you see how talented they are?"

"And I wanna kiss them!" Smudge announced, reaching for the cage.

"Vell, I have to make something!" the chef said.

"Well, cook something else!" Jack said.

"Yeah, cook something else!" Smudge said between kisses.

"EW!" shouted the kissed toads.

But their words came out as "RIBBIT!"

Soon everyone was talking at once. The more they talked, the louder they got.

Except Carlos. He was too depressed to talk. He was going to be a toad forever.

Suddenly a new voice entered the discussion. A bold, authoritative voice.

"What is going on here?"

Pinky, Jack, Smudge, Chef Auskotzen, and the toads fell silent. Standing in the doorway to the kitchen were two figures. One was tall and lean, the other was short and round. It was the king and queen.

"I said," King Carmine spoke again, "what is going on here?"

Jack cleared his throat. "Well, you see, Your Majesty—"

But the old jester was interrupted by

Queen Cora's shriek of surprise. "Carlos!"
she cried.

She raced to Pinky and plucked Carlos
from the princess's hands. "Oh, my goodness! What happened to you?" the queen
asked.

Before Carlos could utter a "ribbit" of
reply, the queen gave Carlos a lipstick-y kiss
on the top of his warty head.

In an instant, Carlos saw himself grow . . .

. . . and grow . . .

. . . and grow . . .

. . . until he was a jingle-toed jester prince
once again.

Carlos's legs were a little wobbly. His

butt ached from all of the hopping. And that cockroach he had eaten was now making his stomach do flips. But he didn't care.

"I'm a person! I'm a person again!" Carlos exclaimed.

Then he paused.

"But wait. *How* did I become a person again?" he asked. "I thought I needed to be kissed by a princess. On the lips. Who loves me with the warmth of two thousand suns."

"Oh, no, sweetie," the queen replied with a laugh. "That's the way to break a *frog* spell! You were a *toad*. To break a toad spell you need to be kissed by the first person who *ever* loved you. And I loved you, Carlos, before you were even born."

"But how did you know it was me?" Carlos asked.

"A mother *always* knows," the queen replied.

Without another word, the queen gripped Carlos in a supersqueezy hug. For the first time in forever, Carlos didn't mind the hug that much.

The king regarded the happy scene for a long, thoughtful moment. "Carlos?" he said.

"Yeah, Dad?" (Carlos's voice was a little strained because he was still being hugged.)

"Knowing how to break magic spells is a

very important part of prince training," the king said.

"I can see why," Carlos replied.

"At your age, you should already know how to break magic spells," the king continued.

"Oh. Okay," Carlos said.

"It takes a lot of time to acquire that knowledge," the king said. "A lot of study. A lot of training."

"Okay . . . ," Carlos repeated. He didn't like where this conversation was going.

"Do you see where this conversation is going?" the king asked.

"No," Carlos fibbed.

The king spoke gently. "I'm saying that I think we need to spend a little more time each day on your prince training, son. And, perhaps, a little *less* time on your jester training."

The king let that statement sink in.

"Do you agree with me, son?" the king asked.

It was one of those questions that had only one answer.

"Yes," Carlos sighed.

CHAPTER 11

The next afternoon, Carlos jingle-jangled faster than usual to his jester lesson.

"I'm here!" Carlos called as he jogged through the high, arched doorway. "So let's get started. Dad said I can only stay for an hour today."

At once, Carlos noticed that the Fancy Castle ballroom was more crowded than usual. Standing in a straight line before Jack

the Jester were five toads.

"Meet the new students, kiddo!" Jack said

with glee.

"Are these . . . ?"

"Yup! These guys were almost yesterday's dinner," Jack said. "I'm pleased to report that toad is now—and forever—banned from the Fancy Castle menu!"

"That's good news," Carlos said. And he meant it.

"These talented toads are now jesters in training!" Jack announced. "Every lake, lily pad, pond, and puddle on the continent will soon experience the joy of laughter! Isn't that a great idea?"

Carlos considered this. It *was* a pretty good idea. Carlos knew from personal experience that toads loved to laugh.

"But I have a problem, kiddo," Jack said. "I've never taught a class this size before. I'll need a co-teacher."

Carlos raised an eyebrow. "What are you saying? You want me to teach?"

"Of course!" Jack said. "You're a natural. You've already taught these toads how to mime."

"But I can't teach. I'm still a student," Carlos protested. "I still have more to learn."

"*Of course* you have more to learn," Jack said. "The best jesters *never* stop learning. Heck, *I'm* still learning. I'll be learning for the rest of my life. You'll be learning for the rest of your life, too. But you are ready to teach. You're *more* than ready."

"So you're telling me . . . ?"

Jack nodded. "You're a master jester, son. You've been a master jester for a long, long time. And that's why I want to give you this." Jack reached into a lumpy patchwork bag resting by his jingly feet.

He pulled out the Hammacher Jester jewel-encrusted whoopee cushion.

Carlos gasped.

"This, young'un, is your graduation present." He handed it to Carlos. "You earned it."

"Wow!" To make sure he wasn't dreaming, Carlos gave the cushion a squeeze.

BRAAAAAAAAP!

He wasn't dreaming.

"Master jesters use their skills to teach others how to jester," Jack said. "Do you know why?"

Carlos smirked. "Because it is their *dooooody!*"

Jack smirked back. "That's right! So what do you say, kiddo? Will you help me teach the very first class of jester toads? Will you help me spread the joys of jestering to every corner of the continent and every species on the planet?"

"Okay, I'll teach," Carlos said. "But only if they want me to."

Carlos turned to the attentive toads. "Would you like me to teach you how to jester?"

All five toads boldly ribbitted their reply.

Carlos could no longer understand Toad-ese, but he knew a resounding "YES!" when he heard one.

"All right then, class," he said. "Let's begin."

Carlos smiled. He felt a wave of happiness wash over him.

He also felt a pang of hunger.

No, Carlos thought. *It can't be!*

But it was.

Toad You So!

The jester prince of the happy and peaceful land of Faraway Kingdom had a sudden and unmistakable craving for Cockroach Surprise.

ABOUT THE AUTHOR

Roy L. Hinuss is the authorized biographer of the Charming Royal Family. He is also fond of the occasional fart joke. When he isn't writing about Prince Carlos Charles Charming's many adventures, he occasionally accepts kisses from amphibians.

Don't miss any of the adventures in the Prince Not-So Charming series!